This Topsy and Tim
book belongs to

_____

Topsy and Tim
Have a Birthday Party

By Jean and Gareth Adamson

Illustrations by Belinda Worsley

A catalogue record for this book is available from the British Library

Published by Ladybird Books Ltd
A Penguin Company
Penguin Books Ltd., 80 Strand, London WC2R 0RL, UK
Penguin Books Australia Ltd., 707 Collins Street, Melbourne, Victoria 3008, Australia
Penguin Group (NZ) 67 Apollo Drive, Rosedale, North Shore 0632, New Zealand

008

© Jean and Gareth Adamson MCMXCV
Reissued MMXIV

ISBN: 978-1-40930-061-8
Printed in China

www.topsyandtim.com

It was Topsy and Tim's birthday.
The first thing they saw when they
woke up was a pile of birthday presents.

The postman brought them lots of birthday cards and a package from Granny.

"Happy birthday, twins," he said.
"How did you know it was our
birthday?" asked Topsy.
"I guessed!" laughed
the postman.

After breakfast, Topsy and Tim went into the garden to try out their new roller blades.

"Happy birthday, Topsy and Tim," shouted their friends over the fence.

"How did you know it was our birthday?" asked Tim.

"Because you've invited us to your party this afternoon, silly," said Kerry.

Later, Dad took them to the shops to buy party balloons and candles for their birthday cake.

"Happy birthday, Topsy and Tim," said Mrs Patel.
"How did you know it was our birthday?" asked Topsy and Tim.
"A little bird told me," said Mrs Patel.

When they got home, Topsy and Tim helped to
get everything ready for their birthday party.
Dad showed them how to blow up the balloons.
Then they hung the balloons in bright bunches
round the room.

Topsy and Tim and Dad went into the kitchen to help make the party tea. Mummy showed Topsy how to ice the little cakes. Tim stuck a sweet on top of each one.

Dad was putting sticks into the party sausages. He popped a sausage into his mouth, then gave one each to Topsy and Tim.

"Stop that," said Mummy, "or there won't be any left for the party."

"Can Tim and I put the candles on our
birthday cake?" asked Topsy.
"No," said Mummy. "You're having a surprise birthday
cake, so I'll put the candles on. You can help Dad put
the food on the tea table."

Topsy and Tim enjoyed carrying the wibbly wobbly jellies.

Everything was ready for the party.
Then their friends started to arrive.
Vinda was the first, then Tony Welch.
Stevie Dunton and Andy Anderson came together.
"Here I am," said Kerry. Rai was just behind.

They had all brought birthday
presents for Topsy and Tim.
"Is everyone here?" asked Mummy.
"Everyone except Josie," said Topsy.
"We can't start without Josie," said Tim.
"I think we'd better," said Mummy.

First they played musical chairs. Dad played the music. Each
time the music stopped, they had to find a chair to sit on.
"I've not got a chair," said Topsy.
"You're out then," said Dad. Stevie Dunton won musical
chairs. Mummy gave him a prize.

Next they played Pin the Tail on the Donkey. It was Topsy's favourite game. Tim pinned the tail on the donkey's nose and everyone laughed. Tim laughed too when he saw what he had done.

"Time for one more game before tea," said Mummy.
"We'll play Pass the Parcel."
Just then, the doorbell rang. It was Josie.
"Hooray," said Topsy and Tim.

Josie sat down between Topsy and Tim and the music began.
Every time the music stopped, the one holding the parcel had
to unwrap it a bit more.
"Everybody's won something except me," grumbled Josie.
Then she won Pass the Parcel. "This is a good party," said Josie.

"Time for the birthday tea," said Dad. There was plenty of food for everyone and lots of orange to drink.
"I was thirsty," said Andy Anderson.

Mummy came in with the surprise birthday cake.
"Ooh, it's a dinosaur!" said the children.
The dinosaur had candles
all down its back.

All the children sang "Happy Birthday" and Topsy and Tim blew out their birthday candles with one big puff.

Now turn the page and help
Topsy and Tim solve a puzzle.

Look at the two pictures.
There are eight differences.
Can you spot them all?

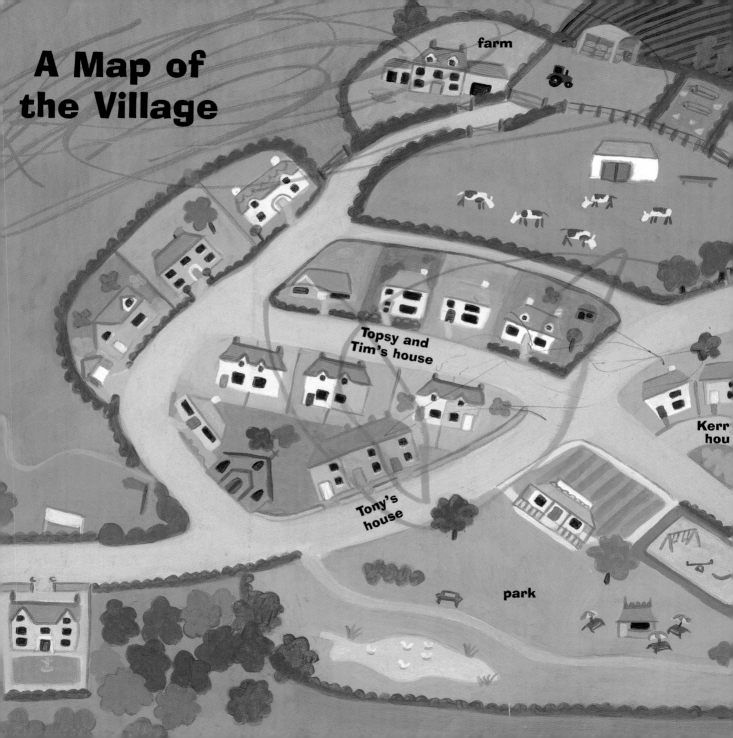

A Map of the Village

farm

Topsy and Tim's house

Tony's house

Kerr hou

park

garage

post
office

health
centre

church

primary school

nursery school

police station

Have you read all the Topsy and Tim stories?

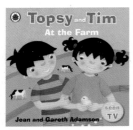
Topsy and Tim: At the Farm
Jean and Gareth Adamson
☐ 9781409303367

Topsy and Tim: Go Camping
Jean and Gareth Adamson
☐ 9781409303336

Topsy and Tim: Go on an Aeroplane
Jean and Gareth Adamson
☐ 9781409300571

Topsy and Tim: Go on a Train
Jean and Gareth Adamson
☐ 9781409304241

Topsy and Tim: Go to Hospital
Jean and Gareth Adamson
☐ 9781409304234

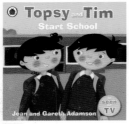
Topsy and Tim: Start School
Jean and Gareth Adamson
☐ 9781409300830

Topsy and Tim: Go to the Doctor
Jean and Gareth Adamson
☐ 9781409303343

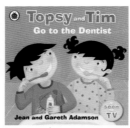
Topsy and Tim: Go to the Dentist
Jean and Gareth Adamson
☐ 9781409300588

Topsy and Tim: Have a Birthday Party
Jean and Gareth Adamson
☑ 9781409300618

Topsy and Tim: Meet Father Christmas
Jean and Gareth Adamson
☐ 9781409311591

Topsy and Tim: Meet the Police
Jean and Gareth Adamson
☐ 9781409308836

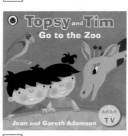
Topsy and Tim: Go to the Zoo
Jean and Gareth Adamson
☐ 9781409300847

Topsy and Tim: Meet the Firefighters
Jean and Gareth Adamson
☐ 9781409307211

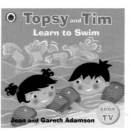
Topsy and Tim: Learn to Swim
Jean and Gareth Adamson
☐ 9781409300601

Topsy and Tim: Play Football
Jean and Gareth Adamson
☐ 9781409303350

Topsy and Tim: Safety First
Jean and Gareth Adamson
☐ 9781409308829

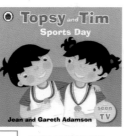
Topsy and Tim: Sports Day
Jean and Gareth Adamson
☐ 9781409309468

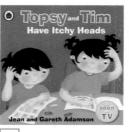
Topsy and Tim: Have Itchy Heads
Jean and Gareth Adamson
☐ 9781409307204

Topsy and Tim: The New Baby
Jean and Gareth Adamson
☐ 9781409300564

Topsy and Tim: Visit London
Jean and Gareth Adamson
☐ 9781409309475

Available on the App Store

The Topsy and Tim app is available for iPad, iPhone and iPod touch.

It is also available on Android devices.